Bennie, the Young Runaway

By
Gaythel Boggs Friend

PublishAmerica
Baltimore

First printing

At the specific preference of the author, PublishAmerica allowed this work to remain exactly as the author intended, verbatim, without editorial input.

ISBN: 1-4137-8147-0
PUBLISHED BY PUBLISHAMERICA, LLLP
www.publishamerica.com
Baltimore

Printed in the United States of America

Dedicated to Onda and Little Larry

Chapter 1

Bennie was small and lean. Grooming and personal hygiene were foreign to him. His red-orange hair was dirty and hung to his lanky shoulders in tangled masses. The boy never owned a toothbrush and seemed to be suffering from a chronic runny nose. His plaid shirt and faded dungarees showed signs of being slept in night after night. Although he seldom wore shoes, on this night he wore his leather high-tops over bare feet.

His parents permitted him to come and go as he pleased. If he was not home when they retired for the night, no big deal. He'd make it home sometime; he always had before, but not this night.

By morning he would be over two hundred miles away from his home in Nevada. Although he was only twelve, he had been providing most of the food and money at his home for months. Neither his Ma nor Pa ever questioned how he got it. No need to, he would have lied anyway. If he was going to do it all, he may as well just do for himself.

"The heck with them lazy bums. I'm ridin' this train as far as it goes," Bennie said aloud to himself as he lay down on the cool wooden floor of the box-car and curled up in the fetal position to sleep.

Bennie had no idea how long he had slept. He was awakened many times during the night by the clacking of the train over the rails. It was way past daybreak. The train had stopped at a rail yard in Wyoming. The sun was casting dust filled rays through the wide cracks on the side of the car. He lay quietly for a while, listening. He could hear birds chirping and cattle bawling. From the distance he recognized the sounds of a city; Model T's clugging and rattling along and an occasional "rugga-rugga" from an impatient motorist.

The only movement was the batting of his eyelids. Bennie did not dare to get up and move about carelessly for fear of being detected by the conductor or someone. He knew he had to be very careful from now on. He was a stranger in this city. It wouldn't be like back home where most people overlooked his pilfering and bumming. Back home they figured that was the only way he was going to get anything to eat or any money either, for that matter. He would steal or bum something from one person and either sell or trade it to someone else. With each transaction Bennie would profit a little more. But pickins' were growing slim there and he figured he'd better move on to greener pastures. What he didn't know was that most of the items he stole or bummed ended up back in the hands of the rightful owners.

When Bennie was certain there wasn't a soul around close enough to the car to either see or hear him he stood up cautiously and stretched his tired achy frame. His eyes felt like they were filled with sawdust. His mouth was dry and his stomach empty.

Bennie wet his lips with his tongue and wiped his nose on his right sleeve, which was stiff and crusty from the elbow to the cuff from previous wipings. He started for the door and stopped abruptly, caught his breath and stared wide-eyed. The door was opened about a foot or so. When he had crawled on board the night before he made sure to close the door tightly behind him. Someone knew he was there and had set a trap for him. They were probably waiting and watching from out there somewhere. They were hidden from his view but were able to see that door and watch for him to emerge. Before he could clear the car they would be on him like ugly on an ape.

Bennie crept to the side of the car and peered through a crack between the rough planks. All he could see was a cattle car across the way, a poor stray hound searching for a scrap of food and an occasional sage brush roll by in a gust of wind and dust. He would have to carefully ease the door open just a few more inches. When this was done he would dash through the door and hit the ground a runnin'.

As Bennie leaped through the door he caught his right arm on something. He felt a sharp pain about midway between his shoulder and elbow. He heard the fabric of his shirt tear. He couldn't let this slow him down. He would run till he was sure no one was about to catch him, then he would stop and inspect his wound.

He ran top speed, jumping tracks and dodging sagebrush. He made it to the edge of the city and raced down a busy, noisy street. He was darting around pedestrians, glancing from side to side, looking for an alley or doorway in which to hide. People stared after him curiously, and then looked to see who was chasing him. There was no one. He had made a clean getaway, but what he was running into could prove to be far worse than what he was running from.

Just moments after the boy made good his escape, the conductor was inspecting his train before departing the yard. He looked into the car where he had seen the boy. He gazed at the empty corner and shook his head slowly. He carried with him two biscuits and ham wrapped in wax paper.

What a pity, he thought. A kid that young out on his own. He turned and looked out over the tracks toward the city and whispered, "Good luck, kid, you're gonna need it."

Chapter 2

Bennie made his way through the city and came to a river. He sat down on a rock and inspected his arm. He had a nasty cut. His sleeve was soaked with blood and was beginning to dry and stick to his arm. He eased his shirt off so as not to start the bleeding again. He stretched out his right leg and leaned back so he could slip his hand into his pocket for his knife. He cut a piece of material from his shirttail and then cut off part of his shoestring. He placed the cloth over the cut and wrapped the string around it and tied it as best he could, using his left hand and his teeth.

After he was satisfied with his bandage he slipped down to the water's edge and dipped a drink in his cupped hands. He then rinsed the blood from his shirt and spread it over a bush to dry. His stomach was growling and his sides ached from all that running.

Moments later Bennie had taken off his shoes and was soaking his feet in the cool water when he heard voices. He slid down behind the tall grass at the river's edge and watched. Two young girls topped the knoll and started down the path toward him. They were carrying canvas tote bags. They did not notice Bennie. Instead they turned and walked up river away from him. He lay still and watched, hoping they would go swimming or something, then he would slip over and see if they had anything worth stealing in those bags. If they just had something to eat that would satisfy him plenty

The girls passed through some willows and were out of sight. Bennie could still hear them giggling and talking and in a while he heard them splashing in the water. He thought he had it made now and started crawling through the grass with his boots tied together and hung around his neck. He got as far as the willows before the two boys came over the bank and spotted him.

"Hey, what do you think you're doing? One of the boys yelled as he bent to pick up a stick. "Get out of here you little brat!"

The boys started running at him. Bennie scampered away just in the nick of time. The boys laughed and disappeared through the willows to where the girls were.

Now Bennie was really in a fix. Not only had he missed out on a possible meal, he had left his shirt behind. "No matter, he said to himself, I needed a new shirt anyway."

Judging from the position of the sun Bennie guessed it to be around noon. He was headed back to town. He had to find something to eat and try to pick himself up a shirt from one of the stores. This was the only time he was thankful he was so small. He could slip into one of the shops behind someone undetected by the owner. He'd get a shirt and put it on and walk out of the store as pretty as you please and no one would notice him. He may even be able to get a pair of socks, too, his feet were getting sore from wearing those boots without any.

Bennie got a shirt and put it on hidden behind a rack of dresses. He looked around for some socks but the only ones he saw were behind the counter. It would be impossible to get them without asking the clerk for help. He gave up on the socks and walked out onto the walk. The shirt was white with blue stripes. Bennie stuck out like a sore thumb with it on.

Bennie walked on down the street and crossed to the other side. He was standing outside a cafe begging for money when a well-dressed elderly lady stopped in front of him.

"What do want money for young man?" she asked.

"I want to get me something to eat." Bennie replied.

"Seems to me you should have bought something to eat instead of that shirt," she said smiling.

Bennie followed her gaze to the price tag still attached to the cuff. He was certain she knew he had stolen it. He was about to turn and run when she laughed and said, "Here, take this and buy yourself a hot meal."

Bennie reached out his hand and she dropped something in it and walked away. He waited till she turned the corner before he looked to see what she had given him. He held in his hand a five-dollar bill.

"Hot Dang!" he exclaimed, as he turned to go into the café. "I can eat a whole week on this!"

Chapter 3

Bennie had never been inside a restaurant before. He stopped inside the door and looked around. There were several people sitting at tables eating. Some of them stopped and stared at him. He felt uncomfortable but his hunger outweighed his fright.

Bennie walked over to a gentleman sitting alone and said quietly, "How does a body go about getting something to eat in here?"

The man looked at Bennie for a few seconds before answering. "You have to have money, kid, food ain't free in here."

"I know that. I have money," Bennie replied, showing the man his five dollar bill.

"Well, just sit down at a table and the waitress will take your order," the man instructed.

"Ain't nobody takin' nothin' from me without a fight," Bennie said.

The man laughed and eyed Bennie even closer. "Sit down here with me," he said, smiling, "I'll show you how to get something to eat."

Bennie did as the man said. Soon a young lady wearing a white dress and a black apron came over and spoke to him and reached him a menu. He took it from her and stared at it as if it were a snake. He had no idea what it was or what to do with it.

The lady told Bennie she would be back later to get his order and walked away to speak to some people at another table. When she returned to Bennie with her pad and pencil and asked if he was ready to order the man at the table intervened.

"Yes, he said, this lad will have the special."

After the waitress left to give the cook Bennie's order the man smiled at him and said, "Always get the special. It's cheap and it is always good."

As the man was leaving he looked over at Bennie, who was at that time being served his meal, and said, "See you around, partner."

"Partner" Wonder what he meant by that?" Bennie thought.

Chapter 4

It was evening and Bennie was looking for a place to sleep that night. He still had four dollars and twenty-five cents. He thought about renting a room but decided to save his money for food. He had not been here long enough to learn where the best places to get a free meal were. He walked on, looking for a shed, barn or an abandoned house.

Bennie was on the outskirts of town when he came upon the man he had met in the cafe. The man saw Bennie approaching and waited for him to catch up to him.

"What you doing out this way, sonny?" he asked.

"Just walkin'," Bennie lied.

"You wouldn't be looking for a place to bed down for the night, now would you?" the man said smiling.

Bennie eyed the man carefully. As far as he could tell he wasn't too prosperous. He remembered what the man had said to him at the restaurant.

"What did you mean when you called me "partner"?," Bennie asked, looking the man straight in the eye.

"Well," the man answered slowly, "Seems to me we are two of a kind. Unless I miss my guess, you are on your own, too. No home, no family, and no money. Am I right?"

Bennie was not one to trust people right off. He learned that at a very early age, but since he and this man seemed to have so much in common he decided to trust him.

"You're right, Bennie answered honestly. I am looking for a place to sleep tonight."

"You got one, follow me," the man said as he left the road and started up a path that led into a wooded area.

Bennie tagged along behind the man. He wondered if there was a house up the way. He realized suddenly that he didn't know the man's name. The man had not asked Bennie what his name was either. Bennie wondered if he should ask him who he was, but decided against it. This man may not want anyone to know who he was. For all Bennie knew he could be some kind of outlaw.

No matter, Bennie thought. He has treated me all right so far. I'm not gonna worry about what he might have done in the past.

Bennie and the man had walked into the woods for some hundred yards or so when they came to a clearing where there was a small shack constructed of bits of lumber, tin and cardboard. There were no windows and when the man led Bennie inside he could tell it had a dirt floor. After Bennie's eyes adjusted to the darkness he could barely make out the man fumbling around in the room. In a few seconds he heard a match strike and there was a light. He blinked and looked around. The man had lit a coal oil lantern and set it on a wooden crate setting bottom up in the middle of the room. There was no other furniture, just some straw piled in one corner with some faded, ragged quilts spread over it. A rope had been stretched across one corner and various articles of clothing were hung over it.

The man tossed Bennie a burlap sack and said, "Better gather some straw before it gets too dark and make you a bed. I'll give you one of my blankets. Ain't much, but it beats sleeping outside."

Bennie was walking about gathering dried grass and leaves and stuffing them into his sack when he came to a deep hollow. He looked over into it and saw some bottles strewn about. He climbed down a ways and picked one up. It was a liquor bottle. There must have been a dozen of them lying around. He tossed the bottle on down into the hollow and climbed back up the hill to finish the task of filling his sack.

After Bennie had constructed his bed in one of the corners of the room he stretched out on it to see how it felt. He crossed his legs and folded his arms over his chest. The bed felt pretty good. In a while the man came back into the room and sat down cross legged, Indian fashion on his bed. Bennie glanced over at him. The man was staring at something he held in his hands. It was a bottle, a liquor bottle. There was only a swallow or two of the amber colored liquid left. The man turned the bottle up and drank it, then tossed the empty container aside and lay down with his back to Bennie.

"Be sure to turn the light out before you go to sleep, boy," the man said. "See you in the morning."

Bennie was not sleepy yet but turned the lantern out and lay back down and covered up. He lay on his back for a long time staring up into the darkness. He thought about his parents and home. He was not any better off here than he was back there, but determined not to go back. He would make it here somehow; he had to.

When Bennie awoke the next morning he was disoriented for awhile before he realized where he was. He stood up and rubbed the sleep out of his eyes and looked around. The man was not in his bed. Bennie figured he had already started walking into town and hurried to catch up to him. He ran almost all the way to town before he saw him. The man was just stepping up onto the sidewalk. Bennie yelled for him to wait but the man quickened his pace and went on. When he got to where he had seen the man he was no where in sight.

Bennie walked down the sidewalk looking for him. He did not understand why the man had run away from him. He gave up trying to find him and went on back up the street to get some breakfast. He felt more confident now that he knew about how to go into a restaurant and eat.

After Bennie finished his ham and eggs he picked up the slip of paper the waitress had left at his table and walked over to pay for his meal. He handed the lady the paper and reached into his pocket for his money. It was not there. He searched every pocket. He did not have one red cent left. He was frantic. He did not know what to do. The lady told him again the amount of his bill. Bennie stared at her for a second then bolted for the door and ran down the street.

Bennie's mind was racing. What could have happened to the money? It must have slipped out of his pocket onto his bed. He hurried back to the shack and searched through the quilt. The money was not there. The man had not returned yet either.

Bennie sat down on the wooden crate and tried to figure out what to do next. He decided to go back into town and search for the man again. As he was walking down the path through the woods he saw the man come into view. Bennie stepped off to the side of the path. The man was staggering and mumbling to himself. After he passed Bennie stepped out quietly and followed him. The man was carrying something. He teetered over to a fallen tree and stuffed the bundle under it and covered it with leaves. Bennie waited till the man was inside the shack before going to investigate the hiding place.

He raked back the leaves with his hands and pulled the package out. Inside was two bottles of the same amber colored liquor like the one he saw the man with the night before.

"So that's what happened to my money," Bennie said with disgust. "That scum stole it to buy this rot gut."

Bennie was furious. He swore to get even.

Chapter 5

With no money and no place to sleep Bennie was right back where he started. He walked around the city till after noon. He had managed to bum some change, but not enough to buy a decent meal. His feet were blistered from walking so much. He decided to go around some of the streets where the homes had clotheslines in the yard. He might luck out and get a pair of socks.

Bennie was sauntering down a beautiful, shady, tree lined street where most of the homes were painted white. He could smell wild honeysuckle in the air. The birds were singing and bees and butterflies were flitting about flowers blooming along white picket fences. If he were going to get anything here he would have to go around to the backs of the houses.

He walked quietly down a pathway between two large two-story homes that led to an alley. He was very careful to keep his eyes open. He never knew where there might be a dog that would alert its master of his presence.

He made it to the rear corners of the homes and scanned the area carefully. He didn't see anyone but he caught a familiar aroma in the air. He could smell apple pie. He looked to his right and there it was, setting on a windowsill. His mouth watered. He stooped over and crept to the window and reached up and touched the pan with a fingertip. The pan was cool enough to carry with bare hands so he grabbed it and started back down the path the way he had come. Just as he turned the corner and started hurrying down the street he heard a woman yell for him to stop. He quickened his pace and kept going. When he got down the street a ways he looked back over his shoulder to see if she was after him. The same woman that gave him the five dollars the day before was coming down the street with a broom in her hand. She recognized the boy by the shirt he was wearing.

Bennie tucked the pie under his left arm and ran as fast as he could. He kept up his pace till he was sure he was out of her sight. When the coast was clear he slowed down and decided to go back to the place he had discovered on the riverbank and eat his pie.

Bennie usually never let his conscience bother him when he stole from someone, but this time he did. That woman had been very generous with a straggly little boy she didn't even know and he repaid her kindness by stealing from her.

Bennie sat on his rock, staring into the water. He went over the day's events in his mind. He felt so alone; so scared. He pulled his legs up and wrapped his arms around his knees. He rested his head on his knees and for the first time since he couldn't remember when, he cried. Deep wrenching sobs that tore the heart right out of him.

Chapter 6

Bennie found an unlocked door on the back of a church and crept in and tried to lie on a bench to sleep that night but it was much too uncomfortable. He ended up sleeping on a mat on the floor. As best as Bennie could recollect this was the first time he had been in a church. When Bennie awoke the next morning he was amazed at how beautiful the stained glass windows were. The bright reds and violets caught the morning sunrays and reflected color all through the building. Bennie thought he had never seen such beauty. He had found a safe place to sleep. Who would ever look for a thief and scoundrel in a church?

As Bennie was sneaking out of the church he noticed blood stains on his sleeve. He had almost forgotten about his cut. He would have to examine it soon. It probably needed a new dressing. He went to his favorite place at the river and took his shirt off. The cloth he had placed on it before was stuck fast. He would have to soak it loose with water. The area around the cut was red, swollen and tender.

Bennie took his boots off and waded out into the water up to his shoulders. He tugged at the bandage till it slipped off. He then washed the cut as well as possible and walked back out on the bank and sat on his rock. Again he cut a piece of material from his shirttail and dried his arm. It was then that he noticed just how bad the cut really was. He thought it might be infected, but put off trying to find a doctor, if there was one in town.

Later Bennie walked around and peeked into all the general stores. There weren't enough shoppers in any of them yet. He would have to wait till later in the day when they were busy so the storekeeper would not notice him. He stepped into an alley and sat in the shadows, waiting. He was looking out to the sidewalk when the man walked by slowly. The man was limping. "Good," Bennie said to himself. "He probably broke his leg. Shame it wasn't his neck."

Shortly before noon Bennie stepped back onto the walk and entered the nearest general store. There were several shoppers milling about. He stayed as far away from the clerk as possible, keeping an eye on him. He poked around for several minutes examining this and that. He would be unable to conceal a number of items. He would have to either make several trips in and out or go to other stores. He decided on the later.

Bennie managed to get a small can opener and two cans of beans from the first store. He hurried to the church and hid the beans behind a loose board under the pulpit. He slipped the can opener into his pocket. He then went back into town to try his luck at one of the other stores. By evening he had succeeded in obtaining quite a haul. He even managed to slip some socks into his pocket.

Bennie returned to the river, took off his boots and soaked his feet in the cool water. When his feet were dried he put on his socks and shoes. His feet sure did feel better.

Bennie spent the rest of the day strolling about town. He still had the change he begged the day before. He would try to get more today. As long as he could steal his food he could save his money.

The next day as Bennie was snooping about one of the general stores a can with a picture of skull and crossbones caught his eye. The can was setting high on a shelf behind the counter. He knew whatever the container held was poisonous. An idea struck him and he smiled. He knew how to get even with that low-life that took his money.

Bennie reached into his pocket for his money and counted it. He had a total of sixty-three cents. That would surely be enough to buy it. He walked over to the clerk, pointed to the can and asked, "How much for that?"

The clerk looked to see what Bennie was pointing to and said, "Thirty-five cents."

"I want it," Bennie answered as he dug into his pocket for his change.

The clerk looked at Bennie for a few seconds. "Do you know what that is?" he asked. "That is lye. Are you sure that is what you want?"

Bennie was apprehensive for a moment. He felt he was going to have trouble getting the man to sell it to him. He had to think fast. He had seen that stuff somewhere before. He remembered. His Ma used it when she used to make soap.

"I don't want it, Ma does," Bennie lied. "She sent me to fetch it."

"Oh, I see," the man said as he stepped upon a stool and took the can of lye down from the shelf.

Bennie paid the man and hurried away with his purchase. He was humming to himself and skipping down the sidewalk. He would sure fix that ole drunk once and for all.

Chapter 7

One morning after breakfast Bennie walked to the outskirts of town to watch for that man. He intended to hide in the woods and wait for him to come along and hide some more liquor. He had checked the other hiding place but found nothing. The man must be hiding his booze somewhere else.

Bennie carried with him the can of lye. He wasn't sure how much to put in a bottle of whiskey so it wouldn't be noticeable by the one drinking it. If he didn't get enough in the first time he would do it again.

It wasn't until the third day of hiding that Bennie caught sight of the man. He was hardly able to walk and Bennie thought he was drunk. The man would take a few feeble steps, fall to his knees and throw up. It took him forever to get back on his feet. With each step the man moaned in pain.

Bennie followed the man, careful to stay hidden. He was about to give up on the man having a bottle when something fell from under his coat. When the man stooped to retrieve it he fell to his knees again. Before trying to get back up on his feet he uncorked the bottle and took a drink. Bennie watched and waited. "Go on, hurry up and hide it," Bennie whispered.

As if the man was obeying Bennies' wish he stopped just outside the shack and stashed the bottle into a hollow stump and went inside and lay down on his bed. Bennie waited for close to an hour before approaching the shack. He wanted to make sure the man was asleep. He was sore afraid of what the man might do if he caught him messing with his liquor.

Bennie got the bottle and slipped down beside the shack and sat down. He eased the cork out and sat the bottle between his feet to steady it. He used his pocketknife to pry the lid off the can and using the blade dipped out some of the gray-white crystals and dropped them into the bottle. He swirled the bottle around to see if the lye would mix with the liquid. It did, so he dropped in a bit more.

"That ought to do it," Bennie said to himself, and corked the bottle and slipped it back into the stump.

Little Bennie knew the man already lay dead on his bed...

Chapter 8

Bennie thought that revenge on the man was justified. He had never imagined it would bother him. As a matter of fact he never thought of what might happen or how he would feel afterwards. He lay awake most of the night. What sleep he did get was filled with tormenting dreams.

When Bennie was strolling down through town he noticed there were very few people and no stores were open. He had no idea what time it was but felt it was not that early. He was wondering if it might be Sunday. Just then the sound of church bells broke the silence. He knew he would not be apt to find and shops open and decided to go to the river till church was over.

Just as Bennie topped the riverbank his foot caught on a vine and he feel face first. He landed about half way down the hill. His arm hurt something fierce. He sat up and clasped his hand over the wound. It felt wet and warm. He pulled his hand away and looked at it. It was covered with blood. He slipped his shirt off and noticed the cut was bleeding profusely. He pulled the crude bandage off and the blood ran down his arm and dripped off his elbow.

Bennie was terribly frightened. He rushed to the water's edge, fell to his knees and bent over to wash the blood from his arm. He was feeling quite ill. He had a time getting the bleeding stopped and redressing his arm. His arm did not seem to be healing at all. It pained him more each day and was filled with a yellow-green substance. Bennie had meant to find a doctor and get it tended to. He vowed to that the very next day.

Due to his queasy stomach and aching head Bennie did not go back into town that day. He lay down on some leaves in the shade of a large tree and went to sleep. He slept peacefully for quite some time, due in part to his weakened state and partly because he had not slept the night before.

The sun was low in the western sky when he awoke. He was burning up although he was lying in the shade. He stood up and nearly fell down from dizziness. He reached out and took hold of a branch to steady himself. His head was aching, his arm was hurting and he felt very strange. He had to get to the church. It would be cooler there. He would rest that night and feel better in the morning.

Bennie staggered and nearly fell several times before he got to the church. Even after he was inside he still felt hot. His brow was beaded with perspiration and his body was damp and his clothes stuck to him. He lay down on the floor and stared up at the ceiling. He could not get comfortable. He sat up and rolled the small mat up and placed it under his head for a pillow and finally drifted off to sleep.

Bennie awakened some time during the night. He was freezing and his teeth were chattering. He knew it was not winter; it was the height of summer. He decided to slip out back of the church and build a fire. He crawled on hands and knees and felt his way to the pulpit. He found his matches and stood up to find his way to the back door. His head was spinning and he reached out to grasp something to steady himself. That was the last thing he remembered till he woke up the next morning.

The sun was casting colorful rays into the room. Bennie had a terrible headache. He lay still for several minutes before trying to get up. His mouth was so dry and his lips were cracked and sore. He did not know what the matter was. He thought if he would eat something he may feel better.

After eating he made his way back down to the river. The river was getting lower and there was quite a bit of mud at the water's edge. Bennie waded out a ways and dipped a drink. The water tasted rancid, but at least it was wet.

By this time Bennie was feeling some better and started back over to the residential area of town and see if he could steal a blanket from a clothesline. He did not want to spend another night freezing. He would stay away from that woman's house. He was ashamed of stealing from her and vowed never to do it again.

As Bennie walked around looking for some laundry hanging out to dry that man crossed his mind often. He wondered if he had drunk the poison. Several times he started to go back and throw the bottle away but did not want to risk being seen up there. As far as he knew no one had ever seen them together except for that time in the cafe.

"Well, look what we have here," Bennie said aloud to himself as he happened upon a home with sheets and blankets flapping in the warm summer breeze to dry.

Bennie scanned the area. He did not see anyone so he crept up to the line, pulled off the pins, rolled the blanket up in his arms and made a bee line back to the church.

After running so hard to get away with that blanket, Bennie was very weak. He lay down and covered himself with the blanket and napped for awhile. Again he was haunted by bad dreams. This time he dreamed that man was chasing him with a broken bottle. The man was slashing at his face with the sharp, ragged edges of the broken glass.

Bennie woke up suddenly and sat straight up. "Why did I do it?" He moaned, holding his head in his hands. "Why?"

Chapter 9

That afternoon Bennie rambled around looking for a doctor's office; found one and stepped inside. A middle-aged man with graying hair and mustache and wearing a white jacket looked up from his desk and greeted him.

"What may I do for you, young man?" Dr. Snyder asked.

"I need something for my cut," Bennie answered, pulling up his sleeve.

The doctor got up from his seat and walked over to examine Bennie's arm. He removed the dressing Bennie had put over it and shook his head. He asked Bennie to please step into the other room.

After Bennie was seated upon the examining table Doctor Snyder stepped over to a cabinet filled with a variety of jars and bottles and picked one up. He then picked up a towel and asked Bennie to hold out his arm. The doctor placed the towel under his arm and said, "This may sting a bit."

"Ouch!" Bennie said. "That hurts."

"This cut is very infected," Dr. Snyder said. "This will help get rid of the infection."

After the doctor had placed a clean dressing on Bennie's arm he instructed him to keep it dry and clean.

When Bennie asked the doctor how much he owed him he said there would be no charge and showed Bennie to the door and watched him go down the street.

Dr. Snyder had never seen the boy. He thought he knew all the people here. Most of the children he had brought into this world. He wondered who this lad was and where he lived. He could not imagine why anyone would allow his child to go so dirty. He opened the door and windows to let in fresh air. Bennie had left a stench in the room.

Suddenly a man burst into Doctor Snyder's office. "Come quick, Doc!" he said breathlessly. "I think I found a dead man!"

"Where?" Dr. Snyder asked.

"In an old shack up in the woods," the man answered.

"Are you sure he's dead?" Doc asked.

"I think so. He looks dead to me," the man replied.

"Wait till I get my bag," Doctor Snyder answered. "He may still be alive."

The man and Dr. Snyder were rushing down the street when they met Bennie going in the opposite direction. He stopped and stared after them. They were going in the direction of the man's shack in the woods. Bennie followed and watched to see where they went. The doctor and the other man cut up over the road bank and into the woods. They were going to that man's shack!

Bennie was scared out of his wits! He hid behind a wagon and waited for the men to come back. In a while the man came rushing back into town and went into the sheriff's office. Bennie wondered what was happening.

The sheriff accompanied the first man back down the street and into the woods. In a few minutes all three men emerged carrying something wrapped in a soiled quilt. As they passed by Bennie he could see they were carrying that man. All he could see was the top of a head, but he recognized it. It was that man. He was dead. Bennie watched as the doctor opened the door to a building and the two men carried the body inside.

Bennie slipped to the side of the building and listened. They were saying something about the dead man. They were going on about him dying a terrible death.

"No man should have to die like this," the doctor said.

Bennie could not bear to hear any more. He put his hands over his ears and burst out running back to the safety of the church.

Chapter 10

Bennie sat in a corner of the church; a small, pitiful, whimpering child. He sat motionless for hours, afraid to move, fighting sleep. Every time he closed his eyes he had visions of that body being carried out of the woods and into that foreboding building. A lifeless form. A life that ended because of his deeds. What a burden for one so young, so alone, to bear.

Before he crawled into that boxcar that evening Bennie dreamed of living a life filled with happiness. Instead he had met with nothing but trouble. He thought he had a rough row to hoe before, now there was no end to his misery. He did not know that every time that train pulled into the station at this place, a man disembarked and walked the streets looking for a small boy. A boy he had seen curled up in a corner of a boxcar sleeping. A boy his heart had gone out to. A boy he hoped to find and help.

Bennie had never gone back to the rail yard. He would hear the shrill whistle of the train in the distance and be tempted to go climb onto another car. He had lucked out the first time but was afraid of being caught if he tried it again. He had heard stories of vagrants. How they were thrown into jail or bound in chains and sent to work camps. He did not want to risk a fate like that.

As long as Bennie stayed around this city he would be constantly reminded of what he had done. He decided to move on and risk being caught anyway. This time he would prepare for the move. This time he would take plenty of provisions with him, including his most prized. His blanket.

Yes, he would leave this place and forget it ever existed.

Chapter 11

Bennie slept very little that night. His arm felt some better but he still felt light-headed at times and his stomach was a bit upset. He figured that was due to being so worried.

Bennie finally managed to get some uninterrupted sleep. He slept late the next day. He was starving when he got up and was tired of eating beans, beef and soup out of cans. He thought he would go into town and see if he could find another restaurant. He could already taste some fried eggs with some bacon or ham. A cup of coffee or tea would sure be a welcome change from the water in the river, too.

Just as Bennie got to the edge of town he met a horse drawn wagon loaded with a wooden box. He knew it was the kind of box people were buried in. He had seen one once when his grandfather died. He stared at the box as the wagon rolled by and wondered if it was that man inside. Even after the wagon was around the corner and out of sight he stood there staring down the street as if he were in a daze.

Bennie returned to the church. He opened a can of soup but could not eat much. He had lost his appetite. He thought he would go to the river. When he arrived he took off his boots, rolled up his britches legs and waded out about

31

half way. The water was even lower than before. He dipped a drink and about gagged. As Bennie was wading back to the bank he lost his balance and fell backwards into the mud. He lay there, bewildered, then burst out laughing. What a sight he was.

"There ain't nothin' to do now but go swimmin'," he said, laughing.

He literally crawled back out into the water and splashed and played till he was exhausted. It wasn't until he was out of the water that he remembered his cut. The doctor had instructed him to keep it clean and dry. He took the dressing off and tossed it aside and lay back in the warm sunshine to rest and dry off.

Chapter 12

The same train Bennie had stole away on sat in the rail yard. The conductor had gotten off and walked into the city, as he had done the last two times his train arrived here. He walked up one street and down the other, careful to look into each alley, hoping to find the small, scraggly, long haired boy. He would not give up till he found him.

He had told his wife about the boy he had seen on the train. He relayed to her how the boy had left before he returned with the sandwiches. He had watched for him, expecting he would show up on his train again but to date he had not seen hide nor hair of him.

Bennie strolled around town looking for something to pack his belongings in. He was leaving that evening. He would climb onto the next train going east. He didn't care where he ended up. He wasn't looking for any place in particular. Just some place different, someplace new. He had learned a valuable lesson. From now on he would be extra careful whom he trusted.

He entered a general store, hidden behind a couple of women. He was poking around here and there, not looking for anything in particular, when he saw a case about two foot long and a foot or so deep. That would be perfect to pack his stuff into, but how was he going to get it without being caught?

While Bennie was waiting his chance to grab the case he stood looking out the window. There was a man with a blue and white cap and a blue coat stopping people and asking them something. As he was talking to them he reached out his hand as if measuring the height of something. Then he would point to his shoulders. Bennie watched for a second then was distracted by a woman asking the clerk for assistance to please help her retrieve something from a high shelf.

Bennie darted to the end of the counter and quietly pulled the valise behind the rack of dresses. He peeked through the garments to see if the clerk still had his back turned to him. He did, so Bennie picked the case up and started for the door. Just as he cleared the door and started down the street he heard a man yell, "Stop, you little thief."

Bennie never looked back. He headed straight for the church to pack and prepare for his new adventure.

Bennie did not notice he passed the man wearing the blue and white cap and blue coat. The man quickened his pace and followed the boy. He watched him go around back of the church. Just as he got to the rear of the building he saw the door closing.

"I've found him," the man whispered to himself as he stepped over to a window and peered inside. Bennie was busy pulling canned food from under the pulpit and placing it in the case and was unaware he was being watched.

After Bennie packed all he had into the case he had room for more and decided to go back to town and try to get a change of clothes. He knew he would have to be extra careful this time. The man that he stole the case from might be watching for him. He was headed out the door when an idea struck him. He snapped his fingers and turned on his heel…he would wait till dark and break in and take anything he wanted and still have plenty of time to catch a train.

When he turned quickly on his heels his head began to spin. He sat down on the first pew and held his head in his hands. When he was feeling better he unfolded his blanket in the corner and lay down for a nap. He had no sooner lain down than his stomach began to churn and he barely made it to the door in time. His head was really spinning now and he crawled back to his pallet and lay down again. His stomach began to cramp again. Always before the cramps went away just about as soon as they started but this time they were much worse and lasted longer.

Bennie curled up in a knot on his side and moaned in pain. He felt so hot and his mouth was dry.

"I need some water," he moaned, as he struggled to get to his feet. He wanted to go back to the river but was too weak to walk. He fell to his knees, holding his stomach with one hand and using the other to aid in crawling. He made it to the river and lay down and drank like a thirsty animal. Thinking he would be all right shortly, he rolled over on his back in the grass. The treetops and sky were going in circles. He closed his eyes to blot them out and drifted off to sleep.

Bennie was awakened suddenly by a heindish laugh. He could see the bulk of a man between him and the sun. He squinted his eyes and moved his head from side to side to see who was standing over him. He screamed in terror. It was that man. That man he had poisoned.

Bennie tried to get to his feet and run but he could not move a limb. The face drew nearer and nearer.

"Tried to do me in, huh, lad," the man said. "Well, it will take more than the likes of a scrawny kid like you to do away with me."

The man laughed that horrible laugh again and drew nearer still. His breath smelled of whiskey and his flesh held a rotting stench.

Bennie jumped and woke himself up. He sat up suddenly and again he was dizzy. Another haunting dream. Would they ever stop? He stood up slowly and started back to the church. His stomach still ached. His head was still spinning. He had to get back and lie down and cover up. He was beginning to chill again.

Mr. Brewster was still waiting for Bennie to come back to the church. He had gone to find someone to go on with the train. Afterwards he returned to talk to Bennie and had found the church vacated. He found the case and knew the boy would be returning so he waited.

Mr. Brewster watched Bennie enter the church and wondered what was wrong with him and hurried to investigate. When he eased the door open and peered inside his heart went out to the poor lad. Never in his life had he seen anything or anyone so pitiful. The boy was lying on the hard wooden floor on a soiled blanket. His little body was shaking and covered with perspiration. The boy was restless, turning his head from side to side and mumbling incoherently. It was obvious the child was sick and burning up with fever.

Mr. Brewster knelt beside Bennie and spoke to him softly. Bennie did not respond. He continued to thrash about and gasp for breath.

Mr. Brewster rushed to find a doctor to come and examine Bennie. He was not sure what illness the boy had but felt it was serious. Luckily the doctor could get away from his office and rushed to the church with Mr. Brewster.

Doctor Snyder recognized Bennie's symptoms instantly and told Mr. Brewster the boy was suffering from Typhoid fever. Mr. Brewster asked the doctor to do all he could for the boy and he would stand good for the bill.

Mr. Brewster rented a room at the hotel so he could nurse the boy back to health. He telephoned his wife explaining he had found the boy. He told her of the boy's illness and stated "They" would be home as soon as the boy was well enough to travel.

Bennie was gravely ill and a few times Dr. Snyder and Mr. Brewster questioned if he would survive. Bennie kept repeating over and over that he was sorry about killing that man. He also said the man stole his money and he was just getting even.

One evening while the doctor was at the hotel to examine Bennie, redress the cut on his arm and leave more medicine with Mr. Brewster Bennie was very delirious.

"What is he saying?" Dr. Snyder asked Mr. Brewster.

"I don't know what he is talking about," Mr. Brewster replied. "He keeps going on about killing a man and how sorry he is. Says the man stole money from him."

"Hum" Dr. Snyder said. "That's interesting. When he comes around we should ask about this. Could be nothing, just a nightmare. But, he may have killed someone before he came here. After all, we don't know who he is or where he came from."

Mr. Brewster did not tell the doctor about Bennie coming into town on the train, and that he suspected that he was from Idaho. Secretly he hoped to keep the boy. If the boy was in trouble before there was probably a good reason. He also hoped the boy was orphaned. If he did have parents they weren't deserving of a child as far as he was concerned. Many questions rumbled around in Mr. Brewster's mind. Questions that could not be answered until the boy was well enough to talk.

One evening of the third week the fever Bennie had began to break and his temperature dropped considerably. The rash on his trunk was slowly fading away. Mr. Brewster was able to get Bennie to drink a whole cup of chicken broth instead of just a few spoons full as before. It seemed the boy was going to recover.

Bennie was very weak on the few occasions he was awake and did not speak much. Mr. Brewster talked to him softly. He told the boy who was caring for him, where they were and urged him not to worry, everything would be all right.

By the fifth week Bennie was out of the woods completely. He was still weak but the fever was gone and he was eating well. He was not sure whether he should trust Mr. Brewster but under the circumstances he did not have much choice. This man had saved his life. He told Mr. Brewster his name and about his parents.

"Pa was nothin' but a lazy bum." Bennie said with a touch of disgust in his voice. He wouldn't strike a lick at a snake. Ma did what she could. Sometimes she would clean house for people or do their washin' and ironin'. She didn't do that too often though,Bennie continued. "She's mighty puny."

"Would you like to come live with me and my wife," Mr. Brewster asked. "I will contact your parents and let them know where you are. You don't have to answer now. Just think about it."

Mr. Brewster did want to take the boy home and raise him as his own. In the twenty-three years he and his wife had been married there were no children. They had wanted children desperately. Already Mr. Brewster was forming a plan in his mind to have an heir. He hoped desperately that Bennie would decide to come home with him.

A knock on the door interrupted Mr. Brewster's thoughts. Dr. Snyder entered the room and he and Mr. Brewster talked for awhile then both walked over and seated themselves on wooden straight back chairs next to the bed where Bennie lay.

"Son," The doctor said, "While you were so ill and delirious you were talking quite a bit. You were going on about killing a man because he stole money from you. Would you care to tell us about it, or can you remember?"

Bennie stared at the doctor for a few seconds then looked at Mr. Brewster. Mr. Brewster smiled and nodded his head.

"It's alright, son," Mr. Brewster assured Bennie. "What you tell us will go no farther than this room. You have my word on that."

Bennie welcomed the idea of unloading his awful secret. He wanted so much to have a real friend to confide in and share things with. He decided to tell the Doctor and Mr. Brewster the truth about that man. He took a deep breath and let it out slowly.

"I did kill a man," he confessed. "I poisoned that man you and the sheriff carried out of that old shack in the woods. I put poison in his whiskey because he stole my money."

The doctor did remember the man. He also remembered the man had died as a result of snakebite. He was sure of it.

"No, boy, no," Dr. Snyder said. "You didn't kill that man. He died from a snakebite. Rattlesnake, if I don't miss my guess. I've seen many a snakebite. It was snakebite alright."

"Are you sure?" Mr. Brewster asked.

"Positive," Doctor Snyder replied.

Bennie thought for a minute. His mind raced back to the time he was sitting in the alley when the man walked by limping. He remembered the last time he had seen him. The same day he slipped the lye into his bottle of whiskey. He thought the man was just drunk but now he realized the man had been terrible ill. What a relief. He wasn't a murderer after all. This good news would change his whole life. He would not be tortured by those terrifying nightmares anymore.

Chapter 13

Mr. Brewster filled a large tub in the water closet adjoining Bennie's room with warm water. Bennie sat on the edge of the bed and watched. He knew what it was but for who was it intended?

Bennie did not have to wonder long. Mr. Brewster cleared his throat and told Bennie to get out of his nightshirt and into the tub.

"You wash good all over. Your head, too. I'll be back in a little while with some new clothes for you," Mr. Brewster said, as he left the room and closed the door.

Bennie was not accustomed to bathing. He slowly walked over to the tub, slipped his nightshirt over his head, slung it over the back of a chair and stepped into the water. The water felt good and he eased down in it and just sat there quietly for a few minutes.

After awhile he began lathering himself all over. He closed his eyes, held his breath and slipped down under the water to rinse. Afterwards when he stood to dry with the large soft towel lying on the stand next to the tub, he changed his mind and sat back down in the water and bathed all over again.

Bennie was really enjoying his bath.

"This is fun," he said. "I ought to do this more often."

When Mr. Brewster returned to the room Bennie had finished his bath and was sitting on the edge of the bed wrapped in a towel. Mr. Brewster handed him a bundle wrapped in brown paper and tied with a cord.

"Here," Mr. Brewster said. "Go over behind that screen and see if these fit. Be sure to put on the underwear, too," he added with a chuckle.

A few minutes Bennie emerged from behind the screen grinning from ear to ear. He turned in a complete circle slowly showing off his new clothing.

Mr. Brewster would not have known it was the same boy he picked up off the floor of the church and carried to that room. Bennie could stand to put on a few pounds, but with Mrs. Brewster's cooking that would not take long,

"Now, Bennie," Mr. Brewster said. "We have two more things to do then we will go to the restaurant and order two of the largest steaks they have."

Bennie did not ask what the two things were. He trusted this kind man and went along with his wishes. Mr. Brewster pulled from his pocket a small brush and a small can of tooth powder and reached them to Bennie. Bennie took the items and walked over to the basin and for the first time in his life, brushed his teeth. He wasn't sure just how to go about doing it, but he did the best he could. His mouth felt fresh and tingly. That, too, he thought, was not so bad.

"What's next?" Bennie asked. "A haircut?"

"Yes, my son," Mr. Brewster answered. "a haircut and a steak dinner."

Mr. Brewster laid his arm across Bennie's shoulders and they were both smiling as they left the room and walked down the stairs, through the lobby and out onto the sidewalk toward the barber shop.

It wasn't until after Bennie was seated at a table in the restaurant that he remembered the time he did not have the money to pay for his breakfast that morning. He wondered if anyone would recognize him. He hoped not. Actually, he hardly recognized himself when he looked into the mirror at the barbershop after his haircut.

Bennie and Mr. Brewster talked quietly while they ate their meal. Mr. Brewster described his ranch to Bennie. The ranch was small, around three hundred acres. Plenty of good grazing land for what cattle he owned.

Mr. Brewster asked Bennie if he knew anything about ranching. Bennie said he never lived on one but used to watch some of the ranchers near where he lived. He had dreamed of one day owning a ranch. He loved horses although he never got any closer than petting one on its velvety nose through

40

the fence.

Bennie told Mr. Brewster he would love to help him on the ranch. Although he was not well educated he was not lazy. All he needed was for someone to give him a chance. He would show Mr. Brewster he was worth his time and trouble.

"I'll try to make you proud of me, Mr. Brewster," Bennie said. "I'll work real hard. You'll see."

Mr. Brewster was proud already and said, "Bennie, all you have to do is try. As long as you do your best that is all anyone can ask, but, you know one day we will have to let your parents know where you are."

Bennie did not know how to respond to that. He would have to wait and see what happened.

After supper Mr. Brewster and Bennie walked around the city talking. Mr. Brewster was planning to leave the next day for home. He had been in touch with his wife that morning by phone to tell her of his plans. Mrs. Brewster told her husband she had prepared a room for Bennie. Although she had never seen the boy she bought him some clothes guessing his size from the description her husband gave her. She was as anxious as her husband to have Bennie come live with them.

Chapter 14

"This sure beats riding in the box-car doesn't it?" Mr. Brewster said teasingly.

Bennie laughed. "Sure does."

Since Mr. Brewster had a few more days left on his leave of absence he rode in the passenger car with Bennie. Bennie was experiencing so many mixed feelings. He was happy and sad at the same time. Happy for himself, happier than he had ever dreamed but sad for his mother. He did miss her at times. He wondered if she was well. Was she going hungry? Bennie figured his father would do what he had always done, which was nothing.

Bennie decided silently to agree to go see his mother if Mr. Brewster brought the matter up again. He hoped it would be soon. That's odd, he thought, as he leaned back in the seat and closed his eyes. I didn't think I would ever want to go home again.

During the ride from the rail yard to Mr. Brewster's ranch Bennie was amazed at how different the countryside looked. There were rolling hills and green pastures with grazing cattle. It was a beautiful country.

Elva ran out to the drive to meet her husband and Bennie. She smothered

Mr. Brewster with hugs and kisses then turned to Bennie and hugged him, too.

"I'm so glad you're home," she squealed. "Come in, come in. I have supper all ready for you."

Mrs. Brewster then put an arm over Bennie's shoulders and ushered him inside the large farmhouse.

Again Bennie was amazed. The home was beautiful. The kitchen was spacious with lots of sparkling windows to let plenty of sunshine in. The aroma of spices and fresh baked bread filled the room. The dining table was laden with an abundance of vegetables, bread, and meat. A large pitcher of milk set on one corner of the table.

Mr. Brewster showed Bennie to the wash room to clean up before he sat down to eat. A habit he was not accustomed to.

Elva Brewster kept piling meat and vegetables onto Bennie's plate. He ate till he thought he would burst. Then afterwards she insisted he eat a large portion of cherry pie. The pie brought back memories of the kind lady his mother used to work for. She often gave him a piece of cherry pie when he was little and went to work with his mother.

"Is something the matter, Bennie?" Mr. Brewster asked.

"No, Sir," Bennie lied.

"Hum," Mr. Brewster said. He knew Bennie wasn't being completely honest.

Later Mr. and Mrs. Brewster showed Bennie around the ranch and introduced him to some of the animals. There were chickens, geese, turkeys, pigs, several cats and a dog. Bennie recognized the dog as the same one he had seen at the rail yard that morning. Mr. Brewster had rescued the dog, too.

The three walked around for awhile. They toured the barn and stables. Mr. Brewster promised to teach Bennie to ride a horse. He was thrilled.

Elva excused herself and returned to the house to tidy the kitchen. Mr. Brewster then asked Bennie if he was homesick.

"Yes, sir. How did you know?" Bennie asked.

"Just guessing," Mr. Brewster answered. "We can go see your mother any time you want. I don't have to go back to work for another week. Any time you are ready just let me know."

"I will," Bennie replied.

The room Elva prepared for Bennie was just off the kitchen to the rear of the house. She selected this room a purpose so if he got hungry during the night food would be nearby.

The bed was full size with a matching bedside table. A tall oak wardrobe stood across one corner. There were two windows that reached almost to the ceiling with pale blue sheers tied back with blue braided ties with tassels.

Bennie admired his room. It was even nicer than the room he stayed in at the hotel when he was so ill. Mom would sure like a room like this, he thought as he undressed and pulled the white chenille spread down and climbed into bed.

When Bennie awoke the next morning he could hear the soft murmur of voices. Mr. and Mrs. Brewster were already up talking over coffee. In the distance a rooster crowed. Although the sun was just peeking over the mountaintop the farm was alive and bustling. Pigs squealed to be fed and cows mooed softly waiting to be milked.

Bennie felt peaceful and lay quietly for several minutes enjoying the sounds. He felt secure and at home. Again his mother crossed his mind. He wondered if she ever woke up in the morning feeling this good.

Bennie walked to the barn with Mr. Brewster and watched as he milked the cows. Mr. Brewster said to pay close attention because the next morning he would learn to milk them critters, as he called them. Milking each morning and evening would be one of his chores once he went back to work. Up until now Elva had done it by herself. Now she would have help.

On the way back to the house Bennie said he would like to go see his mother as soon as they could go.

"Sure thing," Mr. Brewster said. He wanted to get this trip over with. He had grown very fond of the boy as had Elva. They had talked till late the night before. Unbeknown to Bennie, Elva had already learned the boy's address through a friend living near where Bennie was born and raised. This friend had also told Elva that Bennie's father had left shortly after Bennie did. No one knew where he was. Few cared. The only thing people were concerned about was Bennie's mother. Her health had worsened since Bennie left.

Mrs. Brewster's friend had gone to visit Bennie's mother soon after she learned Bennie was going to be living with the Brewster's. She told the ailing woman she had news about her son and that he was doing well.

"I'm sure you will be hearing from him soon," The woman comforted her.

During Breakfast Mr. and Mrs. Brewster and Bennie discussed the trip to visit Bennie's mother. Elva said she could get the Hoffman's next door to take care of the ranch while they were away. They decided to take care of all the necessary arrangements that day and leave soon after church services the following day.

"Church?" Bennie asked.

"Yes, church," Elva said sternly. "We are all going. I bought you a suit. It's hanging in your wardrobe."

Bennie knew there was no use to argue the matter farther. He didn't really want to anyway. The Brewster's had already done so much for him. If they wanted him to go to church with them it was little enough for him to do.

Chapter 15

Bennie did not hear much of the sermon preached that morning. He kept going over in his mind what he would say to his mother. He worried she would be angry with him. He knew she had every right to be. Before he left she had depended on him a great deal. She was not able to do much outside the home. It took all her energy to take care of her own home, careful to stay out of the way of her abusive husband.

Mrs. White never fussed at Bennie for staying away from home so much. She feared if he was under foot all the time her husband would become abusive to him. She knew if this happened she would be powerless to help her son.

As the Brewster's and Bennie were leaving the church a woman came rushing up to Elva all out of breath.

"Elva, Elva," she panted, "Thank God I got here in time. I have a message for you from a woman in Idaho."

This woman, a friend of Mrs. Brewster's, was the operator of the local telephone switchboard. She knew Elva would be in church so she took the call and promised to get a message to her.

"What is it, Dorothy?" Elva asked, her eyes showing great concern. The only person she knew in Idaho was Sister Abigail, the friend she called previously to get information abut Bennie's parents.

The woman took Elva aside and relayed the message to her. Bennie stood with Mr. Brewster. He wondered what they could be talking about. He looked up onto Mr. Brewster's face. He, too, had a worried expression.

"What's wrong?" Bennie asked, fear rising in his voice.

"I'm not sure," Mr. Brewster replied.

Elva thanked the woman, bid her good-bye, and then walked slowly back to where her husband and Bennie stood anxiously waiting for her. She had tears in her eyes and her lips were trembling. Mr. Brewster stepped out and took her hand.

"Is it what I think it is, Elva?" he asked. "Is she…"

"No, not yet," Elva answered. "But she has taken a turn for the worse. If we hurry we may make it in time. Sister Abigail is sitting with her. The doctor has done all he can do."

"Well, we better prepare Bennie," Mr. Brewster said. "We can't keep this from him any longer. He has to be told his mother may be dying."

Bennie took the news better than the Brewster's thought he would. Either that or he was putting up a brave front. Either way he said he knew she had not been well for a long time.

"How's Pa?" Bennie asked.

"Your Pa left soon after you did," Mr. Brewster said. "He just walked out one day. No one knows where he is."

"Figures," Bennie said bitterly.

Bennie was very quiet during the ride back to his home. He was feeling guilty for running away from home. He hoped they would make it in time for him to tell his mother how sorry he was. Maybe he could have helped her. Maybe she wouldn't be so sick.

"Bennie," Mr. Brewster said. "You're awfully quiet. Is there something you would like to talk about?"

Bennie remained silent for a while longer. Finally he answered, his voice strained.

"It's my fault. If I had not run away Ma would be okay."

Mr. Brewster's heart went out to the boy. He guessed he might be feeling guilty. Feeling it was his fault his mother was so ill.

"No, no, Bennie," he said, "Your leaving did not make your mother so ill.

She was not well for years. There wasn't anything anyone could do."

There was little conversation during the remainder of the trip. Elva would point out some landmark or animal and comment on it to Bennie and her husband. They stopped whenever necessary to get something to eat and fill the fuel tank on the automobile. They were all growing tired but kept going. In late afternoon Bennie leaned his head over on Elva's shoulder and fell asleep. She put her arm around his shoulder and kissed the top of his head.

Chapter 16

Sister Abigail met them at the door. They stepped inside the small, dank dwelling cautiously. They did not know what they would find there. All were fearful. Was the woman still alive?

Mr. Brewster motioned for Bennie and Elva to stay put as he followed the sister into the bedroom. He turned to look at them, the late evening sun behind them casting their shadows across the bare floor.

Elva had one arm over Bennie's shoulders and the other across his chest. She could feel his heart pounding rapidly. Just as Mr. Brewster entered the bedroom Bennie leaned his head over against her and closed his eyes. Elva could see his lips moving. He was whispering a prayer. She lowered her head, closed her eyes and did the same.

Sister Abigail and Mr. Brewster stepped over to the woman lying in the bed. The covers were tucked around her shoulders, her eyes closed.

"Mrs. White," he said softly. "Mrs. White, can you hear me? This is Mr. Brewster. I have brought your son to see you."

There was no answer from the woman in the bed. No sign of life within her. Mr. Brewster reached down with a trembling hand and gently touched her forehead. The body was so still. Still and the color of death. Mr. Brewster pulled his hand back slowly. Tears stung his eyes. He turned to the sister. She felt for a pulse. There was none. She shook her head then carefully eased the blanket over the eternally sleeping woman's face.

"God, give me strength," Mr. Brewster whispered. "Give me the words to comfort that poor lad out there. Help me to help him understand. Amen."

Mr. Brewster stepped slowly back into the room where his wife and Bennie were waiting. He stopped and looked at the two, searching for the words to tell the boy his mother had passed on.

Bennie looked onto Mr. Brewster's face. His eyes filled with tears. He nodded his head slowly, knowingly and slipped from Elva's arms. He turned and walked back down the path to the road. There he stopped and waited, with his back to the house, for Mr. and Mrs. Brewster.

People came from miles around. Some drove, some walked, some came on horseback. Others started out with horse-drawn wagons and by the time they reached the church had filled their wagons to capacity with people along the way.

Bennie was amazed. Strangers with sad, friendly faces hugged him and God Blessed him till he was weary. Well-wishers shook hands with the Brewster's and after the funeral a donation of a great sum of money was given to Mr. Brewster to be used in whatever manner he saw fit for Bennie.

Slowly the crowd dispersed. A lone woman was standing next to the Brewster's motor car. She held in her hands a worn Bible. Bennie recognized the lady as one his mother used to work for. She was a kind lady and had always been a friend to his mother.

"Bennie," the woman said. "I have something for you from your mother."

Bennie went to the woman.

She handed him the Bible and said," Inside you will find a letter your Mother wrote for you and left with me in case she passed away before you returned."

Bennie took the Bible. His Mother's Bible, and held it in trembling hands.

"Thank you," he whispered as he walked away to be by himself to read the words his mother had written to him.

My dear Son,

It is my hearts desire that you be happy. I was so worried when you first left home, then I received word that you were going to be making your home with Mr. and Mrs. Brewster. I am so happy for you. I am sorry I could not have done better by you, but know this. I love you with all my heart. I forgave you long ago for anything you may have done wrong. Now, you forgive yourself and live. You live just as much as you can.

Love, Mom

When Bennie returned to the church the Brewster's were waiting for him.

"Are you ready to go home now?" Mr. Brewster asked.

Bennie looked back over his shoulder to the flower-covered grave.

"Bye, Mom," he said. "Thank you. I love you, too."